DR. FAUSTUS

DR. FAUSTUS

Christopher Marlowe

Published 2024 by Gildan Media LLC
aka G&D Media
www.GandDmedia.com

Front cover design by David Rheinhardt of Pyrographx

Interior design by Meghan Day Healey of Story Horse, LLC

Library of Congress Cataloging-in-Publication Data is available upon request

ISBN: 978-1-7225-0381-9

10   9   8   7   6   5   4   3   2   1

DR. FAUSTUS

Dramatis Personæ

THE POPE.

CARDINAL OF LORRAIN.

EMPEROR OF GERMANY.

DUKE OF VANHOLT.

FAUSTUS.

VALDES and CORNELIUS,
  Friends to FAUSTUS.

WAGNER, Servant to
  FAUSTUS.

Clown.

ROBIN.

RALPH.

Vintner.

Horse-Courser.

Knight.

Old Man.

Scholars, Friars, and
  Attendants.

DUCHESS OF VANHOLT.

LUCIFER.

BELZEBUB.

MEPHISTOPHILIS.

Good Angel.

Evil Angel.

The Seven Deadly Sins.

Devils.

Spirits in the shape
  of ALEXANDER
  THE GREAT, of his
  Paramour, and of
  HELEN OF TROY.

CHORUS.

Enter CHORUS

CHORUS

Not marching now in fields of Thrasimene,
Where Mars did mate[1] the Carthaginians;
Nor sporting in the dalliance of love,
In courts of kings where state is overturn'd;
Nor in the pomp of proud audacious deeds,
Intends our Muse to vaunt his heavenly verse:
Only this, gentlemen—we must perform
The form of Faustus' fortunes, good or bad.
To patient judgments we appeal our plaud,[2]
And speak for Faustus in his infancy.
Now is he born, his parents base of stock,
In Germany, within a town call'd Rhodes;[3]
Of riper years to Wittenberg he went,
Whereas his kinsmen chiefly brought him up.
So soon he profits in divinity,
The fruitful plot of scholarism grac'd,[4]
That shortly he was grac'd with doctor's name,
Excelling all whose sweet delight disputes
In heavenly matters of theology;

---

1 Confound. But Hannibal was victorious at Lake Trasumennus, B.C. 217.
2 For applause.
3 Roda, in the Duchy of Saxe-Altenburg, near Jena.
4 The garden of scholarship being adorned by him.

Till swollen with cunning,[1] of a self-conceit,
His waxen wings[2] did mount above his reach,
And, melting, Heavens conspir'd his overthrow;
For, falling to a devilish exercise,
And glutted [now] with learning's golden gifts,
He surfeits upon cursed necromancy.
Nothing so sweet as magic is to him,
Which he prefers before his chiefest bliss.
And this the man that in his study sits!   [*Exit.*]

---

1 Knowledge.
2 An allusion to the myth of Icarus, who flew too near the sun.

Scene I.

*[Enter **Faustus** in his Study.]*

Faustus
Settle my studies, Faustus, and begin
To sound the depth of that thou wilt profess;[1]
Having commenc'd, be a divine in show.
Yet level[2] at the end of every art,
And live and die in Aristotle's works.
Sweet Analytics,[3] 'tis thou hast ravish'd me,
Bene disserere est finis logices.
Is to dispute well logic's chiefest end?
Affords this art no greater miracle?
Then read no more, thou hast attain'd the end;
A greater subject fitteth Faustus' wit.
Bid ὂν καὶ μὴ ὂν[4] farewell; Galen[5] come,
Seeing *Ubi desinit Philosophus, ibi incipit Medicus*;[6]
Be a physician, Faustus, heap up gold,
And be eternis'd for some wondrous cure.
Summum bonum medicinæ sanitas,[7]

---

1 Teach publicly.

2 Aim

3 Logic.

4 The Aristotelian phrase for "being and not being."

5 Greek physician whose theories were highly regarded in the Middle Ages.

6 "Where the philosopher leaves off, there the physician begins."

7 This and the previous quotation are from Aristotle.

"The end of physic is our body's health."
Why, Faustus, hast thou not attain'd that end?
Is not thy common talk sound Aphorisms?[1]
Are not thy bills[2] hung up as monuments,
Whereby whole cities have escap'd the plague,
And thousand desperate maladies been eas'd?
Yet art thou still but Faustus and a man:
Wouldst thou make men to live eternally,
Or, being dead, raise them to life again,
Then this profession were to be esteem'd.
Physic, farewell.—Where is Justinian?   [*Reads.*]
Si una eademque res legatur duobus, alter rem,
     alter valorem rei, &c.[3]
A pretty case of paltry legacies!   [*Reads.*]
Exhæreditare filium non potest pater nisi, &c.[4]
Such is the subject of the Institute[5]
And universal Body of the Law.
His[6] study fits a mercenary drudge,
Who aims at nothing but external trash;
Too servile and illiberal for me.
When all is done, divinity is best;
Jerome's Bible,[7] Faustus, view it well.   [*Reads.*]
Stipendium peccati mors est. Ha! *Stipendium, &c.*

---

1 Medical maxims.

2 Announcements.

3 "If one and the same thing is bequeathed to two persons, one gets the thing and the other the value of the thing,"

4 "A father cannot disinherit the son except," etc.

5 Of Justinian, under whom the Roman law was codified.

6 Its.

7 The Vulgate.

"*The reward of sin is death*." That's hard.   [*Reads.*]
Si peccasse negamus, fallimur, et nulla est in nobis veritas.
"If we say that we have no sin we deceive ourselves, and
    there's no truth in us." Why then, belike we must sin
    and so consequently die.
Ay, we must die an everlasting death.
What doctrine call you this, *Che sera sera*,
"What will be shall be?" Divinity, adieu!
These metaphysics of magicians
And necromantic books are heavenly;
Lines, circles, scenes, letters, and characters,
Ay, these are those that Faustus most desires.
O what a world of profit and delight,
Of power, of honor, of omnipotence
Is promis'd to the studious artisan!
All things that move between the quiet poles
Shall be at my command. Emperors and kings
Are but obeyed in their several provinces,
Nor can they raise the wind or rend the clouds;
But his dominion that exceeds[1] in this
Stretched as far as doth the mind of man.
A sound magician is a mighty god:
Here, Faustus, try thy brains to gain a deity.
Wagner!
    [*Enter* **WAGNER**]
            Commend me to my dearest friends,
The German Valdes and Cornelius;
Request them earnestly to visit me.

_____
1 Excels.

WAGNER
I will, sir.   *Exit.*

FAUSTUS
Their conference will be a greater help to me
Than all my labors, plod I ne'er so fast.
   [*Enter* **GOOD ANGEL** *and* **EVIL ANGEL**.]

GOOD ANGEL
O Faustus! lay that damned book aside,
And gaze not upon it lest it tempt thy soul,
And heap God's heavy wrath upon thy head.
Read, read the Scriptures: that is blasphemy.

EVIL ANGEL
Go forward, Faustus, in that famous art,
Wherein all Nature's treasure is contain'd:
Be thou on earth as Jove is in the sky,
Lord and commander of these elements.
                     [*Exeunt* **ANGELS**.]

FAUSTUS
How am I glutted with conceit[1] of this!
Shall I make spirits fetch me what I please,
Resolve me of all ambiguities,
Perform what desperate enterprise I will?
I'll have them fly to India for gold,
Ransack the ocean for orient pearl,

———————————
1 Idea.

And search all corners of the new-found world
For pleasant fruits and princely delicates;
I'll have them read me strange philosophy
And tell the secrets of all foreign kings;
I'll have them wall all Germany with brass,
And make swift Rhine circle fair Wittenberg;
I'll have them fill the public schools with silk,
Wherewith the students shall be bravely clad;
I'll levy soldiers with the coin they bring,
And chase the Prince of Parma from our land,[1]
And reign sole king of all the provinces;
Yea, stranger engines for the brunt of war
Than was the fiery keel[2] at Antwerp's bridge,
I'll make my servile spirits to invent.
Come, German Valdes and Cornelius,
And make me blest with your sage conference.

    [*Enter* **VALDES** *and* **CORNELIUS**.[3]]

Valdes, sweet Valdes, and Cornelius,
Know that your words have won me at the last
To practice magic and concealed arts:
Yet not your words only, but mine own fantasy,
That will receive no object, for my head
But ruminates on necromantic skill.
Philosophy is odious and obscure,
Both law and physic are for petty wits;
Divinity is basest of the three,

---

1 The Netherlands, over which Parma re-established the Spanish dominion.

2 A ship filled with explosives used to blow up a bridge built by Parma in 1585 at the siege of Antwerp.

3 The famous Cornelius Agrippa. German Valdes is not known.

Unpleasant, harsh, contemptible, and vile:
'Tis magic, magic, that hath ravish'd me.
Then, gentle friends, aid me in this attempt;
And I that have with concise syllogisms
Gravell'd the pastors of the German church,
And made the flow'ring pride of Wittenberg
Swarm to my problems, as the infernal spirits
On sweet Musæus,[1] when he came to hell,
Will be as cunning as Agrippa was,
Whose shadows made all Europe honor him.

VALDES

Faustus, these books, thy wit, and our experience
Shall make all nations to canonize us.
As Indian Moors[2] obey their Spanish lords,
So shall the subjects of every element
Be always serviceable to us three;
Like lions shall they guard us when we please;
Like Almain rutters[3] with their horsemen's staves,
Or Lapland giants, trotting by our sides;
Sometimes like women or unwedded maids,
Shadowing more beauty in their airy brows
Than have the white breasts of the queen of love:
From Venice shall they drag huge argosies,
And from America the golden feece
That yearly stuffs old Philip's treasury;
If learned Faustus will be resolute.

_____

1 Cf. Virgil, Aeneid, vi. 667.

2   Americans Indians,

3 Troopers. Germ. Reiters.

FAUSTUS
Valdes, as resolute am I in this
As thou to live; therefore object it not.

CORNELIUS
The miracles that magic will perform
Will make thee vow to study nothing else.
He that is grounded in astrology,
Enrich'd with tongues, well seen[1] in minerals,
Hath all the principles magic doth require.
Then doubt not, Faustus, but to be renown'd,
And more frequented for this mystery
Than heretofore the Delphian Oracle.
The spirits tell me they can dry the sea,
And fetch the treasure of all foreign wracks,
Ay, all the wealth that our forefathers hid
Within the massy entrails of the earth;
Then tell me, Faustus, what shall we three want?

FAUSTUS
Nothing, Cornelius! O this cheers my soul!
Come show me some demonstrations magical,
That I may conjure in some lusty grove,
And have these joys in full possession.

VALDES
Then haste thee to some solitary grove

---

1 Versed.

And bear wise Bacon's[1] and Albanus[2] works,
The Hebrew Psalter and New Testament;
And whatsoever else is requisite
We will inform thee ere our conference cease.

CORNELIUS
Valdes, first let him know the words of art;
And then, all other ceremonies learn'd,
Faustus may try his cunning by himself.

VALDES
First I'll instruct thee in the rudiments.
And then wilt thou be perfecter than I.

FAUSTUS
Then come and dine with me, and after meat,
We'll canvass every quiddity[3] thereof;
For ere I sleep I'll try what I can do:
This night I'll conjure though I die therefore.

[Exeunt.]

---

1 Roger Bacon.

2 Perhaps Pietro d'Abano, a medieval alchemist; perhaps a misprint for Albertus (Magnus), the great schoolman.

3 Fine point.

Scene II.

BEFORE FAUSTUS' HOUSE.

[*Enter two* **Scholars**.]

1 Scholar
I wonder what's become of Faustus that was wont to make
    our schools ring with *sic probo?*[1]

2 Scholar
That shall we know, for see here comes his boy.
    [*Enter* **Wagner**.]

1 Scholar
How now, sirrah! Where's thy master?

Wagner
God in heaven knows!

2 Scholar
Why, dost not thou know?

Wagner
Yes, I know. But that follows not.

---

1 "Thus I prove"—a common formula in scholastic discussions.

1 Scholar

Go to, sirrah! Leave your jesting, and tell us where he is.

Wagner

That follows not necessary by force of argument, that
    you, being licentiate, should stand upon't: therefore,
    acknowledge your error and be attentive.

2 Scholar

Why, didst thou not say thou knew'st?

Wagner

Have you any witness on't?

1 Scholar

Yes, sirrah, I heard you.

Wagner

Ask my fellow if I be a thief.

2 Scholar

Well, you will not tell us?

Wagner

Yes, sir, I will tell you; yet if you were not dunces, you
    would never ask me such a question; for is not he
    corpus naturale?[1] and is not that mobile? Then

---

1 *'Corpus naturale seu mobile'* (literally, "natural or movable body") was the scholastic
expression for the subject-matter of Physics.

wherefore should you ask me such a question? But that
I am by nature phlegmatic, slow to wrath, and prone
to lechery (to love, would say),if it were not for you
to come within forty foot of the place of execution,
although I do not doubt to see you both hang'd the
next sessions. Thus having triumph'd over you, will set
my countenance like a precisian,[1] and begin to speak
thus:—Truly, my dear brethren, my master is within
at dinner, with Valdes and Cornelius, as this wine, if it
could speak, would inform your worships; and so the
Lord bless you, preserve you, and keep you, my dear
brethren, my dear brethren.   [*Exit.*]

1 Scholar
Nay, then, I fear he has fallen into that damned Art, for
    which they two are infamous through the world.

2 Scholar
Were he a stranger, and not allied to me, yet should I grieve
    for him. But come, let us go and inform the Rector, and
    see if he by his grave counsel can reclaim him.

1 Scholar
O, I fear me nothing can reclaim him.

2 Scholar
Yet let us try what we can do.   [*Exeunt.*]

_____
1 Puritan.

Scene III.

A GROVE.

[Enter **FAUSTUS** *to conjure.]*

FAUSTUS
Now that the gloomy shadow of the earth
Longing to view Orion's drizzling look,
Leaps from th' antarctic world unto the sky,
And dims the welkin with her pitchy breath,
Faustus, begin thine incantations,
And try if devils will obey thy hest,
Seeing thou hast pray'd and sacrific'd to them.
Within this circle is Jehovah's name,
Forward and backward anagrammatis'd,
The breviated names of holy saints,
Figures of every adjunct[1] to the Heavens,
And characters of signs and erring stars,[2]
By which the spirits are enforc'd to rise:
Then fear not, Faustus, but be resolute,
And try the uttermost magic can perform.
Sint mihi Dei Acherontis propitii! Valeat numen triplex
    Jehovae! Ignei, aerii, aquatani spiritus, salvete! Orientis
    princeps Belzebub, inferni ardentis monarcha, et

---

1 Every star belonging to.
2 Planets.

Demogorgon, propitiamus voS, ut appareat et surgat
Mephistophilis. Quid tu moraris? Per Jehovam,
Gehennam, et consecratum aquam quam nunc spargo,
signumque crucis quod nunc facio, et per vota nostra,
ipse nunc surgat nobis dicatus Mephistophilis![1]
[*Enter* MEPHISTOPHILIS, *a* Devil.]
I charge thee to return and change thy shape;
Thou art too ugly to attend on me.
Go, and return an old Franciscan, friar;
That holy shape becomes a devil best.

[*Exit* Devil.]

I see there's virtue in my heavenly words;
Who would not be proficient in this art?
How pliant is this Mephistophilis,
Full of obedience and humility!
Such is the force of magic and my spells.
[*Now*] Faustus, thou art conjuror laureate,
Thou canst command great Mephistophilis:
Quin regis Mephistophilis fratris imagine.[2]
[*Re-enter* MEPHISTOPHILIS *like a Franciscan* Friar].

MEPHISTOPHILIS
Now, Faustus, what would'st thou have me do?

---

1   "Be propitious to me, gods of Acheron! May the triple deity of Jehovah prevail!
Spirits of fire, air, water, hail! Belzebub, Prince of the East, monarch of burning hell,
and Demogorgon, we propitiate ye, that Mephistophilis may appear and rise. Why
dost thou delay? By Jehovah, Gehenna, and the holy water which now sprinkle, and
the sign of the cross which now I make, and by our prayer, may Mephistophilis now
summoned by us arise!"
2   "For indeed thou hast power in the image of thy brother Mephistophilis."

FAUSTUS

I charge thee wait upon me whilst I live,
To do whatever Faustus shall command,
Be it to make the moon drop from her sphere,
Or the ocean to overwhelm the world.

MEPHISTOPHILIS

I am a servant to great Lucifer,
And may not follow thee without his leave;
No more than he commands must we perform.

FAUSTUS

Did he not charge thee to appear to me?

MEPHISTOPHILIS

No, I came hither of mine own accord.

FAUSTUS

Did not my conjuring speeches raise thee? Speak:

MEPHISTOPHILIS

That was the cause, but *yet per accidens*;
For when we hear one rack[1] the name of God,
Abjure the Scriptures and his Savior Christ,
We fly in hope to get his glorious soul;
Nor will we come, unless he use such means
Whereby he is in danger to be damn'd:

_____

1 Twist in anagrams.

Therefore the shortest cut for conjuring
Is stoutly to abjure the Trinity,
And pray devoutly to the Prince of Hell.

FAUSTUS
So Faustus hath
Already done; and holds this principle,
There is no chief but only Belzebub,
To whom Faustus doth dedicate himself.
This word "damnation" terrifies not him,
For he confounds hell in Elysium;[1]
His ghost be with the old philosophers!
But, leaving these vain trişes of men's souls,
Tell me what is that Lucifer thy lord?

MEPHISTOPHILIS
Arch-regent and commander of all spirits.

FAUSTUS
Was not that Lucifer an angel once?

MEPHISTOPHILIS
Yes, Faustus, and most dearly lov'd of God.

FAUSTUS
How comes it then that he is Prince of devils?

---

1 Heaven and hell are indifferent to him.

MEPHISTOPHILIS
O, by aspiring pride and insolence;
For which God threw him from the face of Heaven.

FAUSTUS
And what are you that you live with Lucifer?

MEPHISTOPHILIS
Unhappy spirits that fell with Lucifer,
Conspir'd against our God with Lucifer,
And are for ever damn'd with Lucifer.

FAUSTUS
Where are you damn'd?

MEPHISTOPHILIS
In hell.

FAUSTUS
How comes it then that thou art out of hell?

MEPHISTOPHILIS
Why this is hell, nor am I out of it.
Think'st thou that I who saw the face of God,
And tasted the eternal joys of Heaven,
Am not tormented with ten thousand hells,
In being depriv'd of everlasting bliss?
O Faustus! leave these frivolous demands,
Which strike a terror to my fainting soul.

FAUSTUS

What, is great Mephistophilis so passionate[1]
For being depriv'd of the joys of Heaven?
Learn thou of Faustus manly fortitude,
And scorn those joys thou never shalt possess.
Go bear these tidings to great Lucifer;
Seeing Faustus hath incurr'd eternal death
By desperate thoughts against Jove's deity,
Say he surrenders up to him his soul,
So he will spare him four and twenty years,
Letting him live in all voluptuousness;
Having thee ever to attend on me;
To give me whatsoever I shall ask,
To tell me whatsoever I demand,
To slay mine enemies, and aid my friends,
And always be obedient to my will.
Go and return to mighty, Lucifer,
And meet me in my study at midnight,
And then resolve[2] me of thy master's mind.

MEPHISTOPHILIS

I will, Faustus.   [*Exit.*]

FAUSTUS

Had I as many souls as there be stars,
I'd give them all for Mephistophilis.
By him I'll be great Emperor of the world,

---

1 Sorrowful.
2 Inform.

And make a bridge through the moving air,
To pass the ocean with a band of men;
I'll join the hills that bind the Afric shore,
And make that [country] continent to Spain,
And both contributory to my crown.
The Emperor shall not live but by my leave,
Nor any potentate of Germany.
Now that I have obtain'd what I desire,
I'll live in speculation[1] of this art.
Till Mephistophilis return again.   [*Exit.*]

---

1 Study.

SCENE IV.

A STREET.

[Enter WAGNER *and the* CLOWN.*]*

WAGNER
Sirrah, boy, come hither.

CLOWN
How, boy! Swowns, boy! I hope you have seen many boys
with such pickadevaunts[1] as I have. Boy, quotha!

WAGNER
Tell me, sirrah, hast thou any comings in?

CLOWN
Ay, and goings out too. You may see else.

WAGNER
Alas, poor slave! See how poverty jesteth in his nakedness!
The villain is bare and out of service, and so hungry
that I know he would give his soul to the devil for a
shoulder of mutton, though it were blood-raw.

---

1 Beards cut to a sharp point (Fr. *pic-à-devant*).

Clown

How? My soul to the Devil for a shoulder of mutton, though 'twere blood-raw! Not so, good friend. By 'r Lady, had need have it well roasted and good sauce to it, if I pay so dear.

Wagner

Well, wilt thou serve me, and I'll make thee go like *Qui mihi discipulus*?[1]

Clown

How, in verse?

Wagner

No, sirrah; in beaten silk and stavesacre.[2]

Clown

How, how, Knave's acre![3] Ay, I thought that was all the land his father left him. Do you hear? I would be sorry to rob you of your living.

Wagner

Sirrah, I say in stavesacre.

---

1 "Whoever is my disciple," the first words of W. Lily's "*Ad discipulos carmen de moribus*" (Ode to His Disciples on Morality).

2 A kind of larkspur, used for destroying lice.

3 A mean street in London.

Clown

Oho! Oho! Stavesacre! Why, then, belike if I were your
man I should be full of vermin.

Wagner

So thou shalt, whether thou beest with me or no. But,
sirrah, leave your jesting, and bind yourself presently
unto me for seven years, or I'll turn all the lice about
thee into familiars, and they shall tear thee in pieces.

Clown

Do you hear, sir? You may save that labor; they are too
familiar with me already: Swowns! they are as bold with
my flesh as if they had paid for [their] meat and drink.

Wagner

Well, do you hear, sirrah? Hold, take these guilders.
[*Gives money.*]

Clown

Gridirons! what be they?

Wagner

Why, French clowns.

Clown

Mass, but for the name of French crowns, a man were as
good have as many English counters. And what should
I do with these?

Wagner

Why, now, sirrah, thou art at an hour's warning,
    whensoever and wheresoever the Devil shall
    fetch thee.

Clown

No, no. Here, take your gridirons again.

Wagner

Truly I'll none of them.

Clown

Truly but you shall.

Wagner

Bear witness I gave them him.

Clown

Bear witness I give them you again.

Wagner

Well, I will cause two devils presently to fetch thee
    away—Baliol and Belcher.

Clown

Let your Baliol and your Belcher come here, and I'll
    knock them, they were never so knockt since they
    were devils. Say I should kill one of them, what would
    folks say? "Do you see yonder tall fellow in the round

slop?[1]—he has kill'd the devil." So I should be call'd
Kill-devil all the parish over.
[*Enter two* **DEVILS**: *the* Clown *runs up and down crying.*]

WAGNER
Baliol and Belcher! Spirits, away!   [*Exeunt* Devils.]

CLOWN
What, are they gone? A vengeance on them, they have
    vile long nails! There was a he-devil, and a she-devil!
    I'll tell you how you shall know them: all he-devils has
    horns, and all she-devils has clifts and cloven feet.

WAGNER
Well, sirrah, follow me.

CLOWN
But, do you hear—if I should serve you, would you teach
    me to raise up Banios and Belcheos?

WAGNER
I will teach thee to turn thyself to anything; to a dog, or a
    cat, or a mouse, or a rat, or anything.

CLOWN
How! a Christian fellow to a dog or a cat, a mouse or a
    rat! No, no, sir. If you turn me into anything, let it be

---

1 Short wide breeches.

in the likeness of a little pretty, frisky flea, that I may
be here and there and everywhere. Oh, I'll tickle the
pretty wenches' plackets; I'll be amongst them, i' faith.

WAGNER
Well, sirrah, come.

CLOWN
But, do you hear, Wagner?

WAGNER
How!—Baliol and Belcher!

CLOWN
O Lord! I pray, sir, let Banio and Belcher go sleep.

WAGNER
Villain—call me Master Wagner, and let thy left eye
    be diametarily[1] fixt upon my right heel, with
    quasi vestigias nostras insistere.[2]   [*Exit.*]

CLOWN
God forgive me, he speaks Dutch fustian. Well, I'll
    follow him, I'll serve him, that's flat.   [*Exit.*]

---

1 For *diametrically.*
2 "As if to tread in my tracks."

Scene V.

[*Enter* **Faustus** *in his study.*]

Faustus
Now, Faustus, must
Thou needs be damn'd, and canst thou not be sav'd:
What boots it then to think of God or Heaven?
Away with such vain fancies, and despair:
Despair in God, and trust in Belzebub.
Now go not backward: no, Faustus, be resolute.
Why waverest thou? O, something soundeth in mine ears
"Abjure this magic, turn to God again!"
Ay, and Faustus will turn to God again.
To God?—He loves thee not —
The God thou servst is thine own appetite,
Wherein is fix'd the love of Belzebub;
To him I'll build an altar and a church,
And offer lukewarm blood of new-born babes:
　　　[*Enter* **Good Angel** *and* **Evil Angel**.]

Good Angel
Sweet Faustus, leave that execrable art.

Faustus
Contrition, prayer, repentance! What of them?

GOOD ANGEL
O, they are means to bring thee unto Heaven.

EVIL ANGEL
Rather illusions, fruits of lunacy,
That makes men foolish that do trust them most.

GOOD ANGEL
Sweet Faustus, think of Heaven, and heavenly things.

GOOD ANGEL
No, Faustus, think of honor and of wealth.

[*Exeunt* **ANGELS**.]

FAUSTUS
Of wealth!
Why, the signiory of Emden[1] shall be mine.
When Mephistophilis shall stand by me,
What God can hurt thee, Faustus?, Thou art safe;
Cast no more doubts. Come, "Mephistophilis,
And bring glad tidings from great Lucifer;—
Is't not midnight? Come, Mephistophilis;
Veni, veni, Mephistophile!
    [*Enter* **MEPHISTOPHILIS**.]
Now tell me, what says Lucifer thy lord?

---

1 Emden, near the mouth of the river Ems, was an important commercial town in
Elizabethan times.

MEPHISTOPHILIS
That I shall wait on Faustus whilst he lives,
So he will buy my service with his soul.

FAUSTUS
Already Faustus hath hazarded that for thee.

MEPHISTOPHILIS
But, Faustus, thou must bequeath it solemnly,
And write a deed of gift with thine own blood,
For that security craves great Lucifer.
If thou deny it, I will back to hell.

FAUSTUS
Stay, Mephistophilis! and tell me what good
Will my soul do thy Lord.

MEPHISTOPHILIS
                              Enlarge his kingdom.

FAUSTUS
Is that the reason why he tempts us thus?

MEPHISTOPHILIS
Solamen miseris socios habuisse doloris.[1]

FAUSTUS
Why, have you any pain that torture others?

---

1 "Misery loves company."

MEPHISTOPHILIS
As great as have the human souls of men.
But tell me, Faustus, shall I have thy soul?
And I will be thy slave, and wait on thee,
And give thee more than thou hast wit to ask.

FAUSTUS
Ay, Mephistophilis, I give it thee.

MEPHISTOPHILIS
Then Faustus, stab thine arm courageously.
And bind thy soul that at some certain day
Great Lucifer may claim it as his own;
And then be thou as great as Lucifer.

FAUSTUS
[*Stabbing his arm.*] Lo, Mephistophilis, for love of thee,
I cut mine arm, and with my proper blood
Assure my soul to be great Lucifer's,
Chief lord and regent of perpetual night!
View here the blood that trickles from mine arm.
And let it be propitious for my wish.

MEPHISTOPHILIS
But, Faustus, thou must
Write it in manner of a deed of gift

FAUSTUS
Ay, so I will. [*Writes.*] But, Mephistophilis,
My blood congeals, and I can write no more.

MEPHISTOPHILIS
I'll fetch thee fire to dissolve it straight.   [*Exit.*]

FAUSTUS
What might the staying of my blood portend?
Is it unwilling I should write this bill?
Why streams it not that I may write afresh?
Faustus gives to thee his soul. Ah, there it stayd.
Why should'st thou not? Is not thy soul thine own?
Then write again, *Faustus gives to thee his soul.*
    [*Re-enter* **MEPHISTOPHILIS** *with a chafer of coals.*]

MEPHISTOPHILIS
Here's fire. Come, Faustus, set it on.

FAUSTUS
So now the blood begins to clear again;
Now will I make an end immediately. [*Writes.*]

MEPHISTOPHILIS
[*Aside.*] O what will not I do to obtain his soul.

FAUSTUS
Consummatum est[1] this bill is ended,
And Faustus hath bequeath'd his soul to Lucifer—
But what is this inscription on mine arm?
Homo, fuge![2] Whither should I fly?

---

1 "It is finished."
2 "Man, fly!"

If unto God, he'll throw me down to hell.
My senses are deceiv'd; here's nothing writ:—
I see it plain; here in this place is writ
Homo, fuge! Yet shall not Faustus fly.

Mephistophilis
I'll fetch him somewhat to delight his mind.   [*Exit.*]
    [*Re-enter* **Mephistophiles** *with* Devils, *giving*
    Crowns and rich apparel to **Faustus**, *and dance,*
    and then depart.]

Faustus
Speak, Mephistophilis, what means this show?

Mephistophilis
Nothing, Faustus, but to delight thy mind withal,
And to show thee what magic can perform.

Faustus
But may I raise up spirits when I please?

Mephistophilis
Ay, Faustus, and do greater things than these.

Faustus
Then there's enough for a thousand souls.
Here, Mephistophilis receive this scroll,
A deed of gift of body and of soul:
But yet conditionally that thou perform
All articles prescrib'd between us both.

MEPHISTOPHILIS
Faustus, I swear by hell and Lucifer
To effect all promises between us made.

FAUSTUS
Then hear me read them: *On these conditions following*
First, that Faustus may be a spirit in form and
substance. Secondly that Mephistophilis shall be
his servant, and at his command, Thirdly, that
Mephistophilis shall do for him and bring him
whatsoever [he desires]. Fourthly, that he shall be in
his chamber or house invisible. Lastly, that he shall
appear to the said John Faustus, at all times, in what
form or shape soever he pleases. I, John Faustus, of
Wittenberg, Doctor, by these presents do give both body
and soul to Lucifer, Prince of the East, and his minister,
Mephistophilis; and furthermore grant unto them,
that twenty-four years being expired, the articles above
written inviolate, full power to fetch or carry the said
John Faustus, body and soul, flesh, blood, or goods, into
their habitation wheresoever. By me, John Faustus.

MEPHISTOPHILIS
Speak, Faustus, do you deliver this as your deed?

FAUSTUS
Ay, take it, and the Devil give thee good on 't.

MEPHISTOPHILIS
Now, Faustus, ask what thou wilt.

Faustus

First will I question with thee about hell.

Tell me where is the place that men call hell?

Mephistophilis

Under the heavens.

Faustus

Ay, but whereabout?

Mephistophilis

Within the bowels of these elements,

Where we are tortur'd and remain for ever;

Hell hath no limits, nor is circumscrib'd

In one self place; for where we are is hell,

And where hell is there must we ever be:

And, to conclude, when all the world dissolves,

And every creature shall be purified,

All places shall be hell that is not Heaven.

Faustus

Come, think hell's a fable.

Mephistophilis

Ay, think So still, till experience change thy mind.

Faustus

Why, think'st thou then that Faustus shall be damn'd?

MEPHISTOPHILIS

Ay, of necessity, for here's the scroll
Wherein thou hast given thy soul to Lucifer.

FAUSTUS

Ay, and body too; but what of that?
Think'st thou that Faustus is so fond[1] to imagine
That, after this life, there is any pain?
Tush; these are trifles, and mere old wives' tales.

MEPHISTOPHILIS

But, Faustus, I am an instance to prove the contrary,
For I am damned, and am now in hell.

FAUSTUS

How! now in hell!
Nay, an this be hell, I'll willingly be damn'd here;
What? walking, disputing, &c.?
But, leaving off this, let me have a wife,
The fairest maid in Germany;
For I am wanton and lascivious,
And cannot live without a wife.

MEPHISTOPHILIS

How—a wife?
I prithee, Faustus, talk not of a wife.

---

1 Foolish.

FAUSTUS

Nay, sweet Mephistophilis, fetch me one, for I will have
  one.

MEPHISTOPHILIS

Well—thou wilt have one. Sit there till I come:
I'll fetch thee a wife in the Devil's name.   [*Exit.*]
    [*Re-Enter* **MEPHISTOPHILIS** *with a* Devil
    dressed like a woman, with fireworks.]

MEPHISTOPHILIS

Tell [me,] Faustus, how dost thou like thy wife?

FAUSTUS

A plague on her for a hot whore!

MEPHISTOPHILIS

Tut, Faustus,
Marriage is but a ceremonial toy;
And if thou lovest me, think no more of it.
I'll cull thee out the fairest courtesans,
And bring them every morning to thy bed;
She whom thine eye shall like, thy heart shall have,
Be she as chaste as was Penelope,
As wise as Saba,[1] or as beautiful
As was bright Lucifer before his fall.
Here, take this book, peruse it thoroughly:
                                        [*Gives a book.*]

_____

1 The Queen of Sheba.

The iterating[1] of these lines brings gold;
The framing of this circle on the ground
Brings whirlwinds, tempests, thunder and lightning;
Pronounce this thrice devoutly to thyself,
And men in armor shall appear to thee,
Ready to execute what thou desir'st.

FAUSTUS
Thanks, Mephistophilis, yet fain would I have a book
    wherein I might behold all spells and incantations,
    that I might raise up spirits when I please.

MEPHISTOPHILIS
Here they are, in this book.   [*Turns to them.*]

FAUSTUS
Now would I have a book where I might see all characters
    and planets of the heavens, that I might know their
    motions and dispositions.

MEPHISTOPHILIS
Here they are too.   [*Turns to them.*]

FAUSTUS
Nay, let me have one book more,—and then I have
    done,—wherein I might see all plants, herbs, and
    trees that grow upon the earth.

_____

1 Repeating.

MEPHISTOPHILIS
Here they be.

FAUSTUS
O, thou art deceived.

MEPHISTOPHILIS
Tut, I warrant thee.   [*Turns to them.*]
                                        [*Exeunt.*]

Scene VI.

[*Enter* Faustus *and* Mephistophilis.]

Faustus
When I behold the heavens, then I repent,
And curse thee, wicked Mephistophilis,
Because thou hast depriv'd me of those joys.

Mephistophilis
Why, Faustus,
Thinkest thou Heaven is such a glorious thing?
I tell thee 'tis not half so fair as thou,
Or any man that breathes on earth.

Faustus
How provest thou that?

Mephistophilis
'Twas made for man, therefore is man more excellent.

Faustus
If it were made for man, 'twas made for me;
I will renounce this magic and repent.
        [*Enter* Good Angel *and* Evil Angel.]

GOOD ANGEL
Faustus, repent; yet God will pity thee.

EVIL ANGEL
Thou art a spirit; God cannot pity thee.

FAUSTUS
Who buzzeth in mine ears I am a spirit?
Be I a devil, yet God may pity me;
Ay, God will pity me if I repent.

EVIL ANGEL
Ay, but Faustus never shall repent.   [*Exeunt* **ANGELS**.]

FAUSTUS
My heart's so hard'ned I cannot repent.
Scarce can I name salvation, faith, or heaven,
But fearful echoes thunder in mine ears
"Faustus, thou art damn'd!" Then swords and knives,
Poison, gun, halters, and envenom'd steel
Are laid before me to despatch myself,
And long ere this I should have slain myself,
Had not sweet pleasure conquer'd deep despair.
Have I not made blind Homer sing to me
Of Alexander's love and Enon's death?
And hath not he that built the walls of Thebes
With ravishing sound of his melodious harp,
Made music with my Mephistophilis?
Why should I die then, or basely despair?
I am resolvd: Faustus shall ne'er repent.

Come, Mephistophilis, let us dispute again,
And argue of divine astrology.
Tell me, are there many heavens above the moon?
Are all celestial bodies but one globe,
As is the substance of this centric earth?

MEPHISTOPHILIS
As are the elements, such are the spheres
Mutually folded in each other's orb,
And, Faustus,
All jointly move upon one axletree
Whose terminine is term'd the world's wide pole;
Nor are the names of Saturn, Mars, or Jupiter
Feign'd, but are erring stars.

FAUSTUS
But tell me, have they all one motion, both *situ et
tempore?*[1]

MEPHISTOPHILIS
All jointly move from east to west in twenty-four hours
upon the poles of the world; but differ in their motion
upon the poles of the zodiac.

FAUSTUS
Tush!
These slender trifles Wagner can decide;
Hath Mephistophilis no greater skill?

---

1 "In direction and in time?"

Who knows not the double motion of the planets?
The first is finish'd in a natural day;
The second thus: as Saturn in thirty years; Jupiter in
   twelve; Mars in four; the Sun, Venus, and Mercury
   in a year; the moon in twenty-eight days. Tush, these
   are freshmen's suppositions. But tell me, hath every
   sphere a dominion or *intelligentia*?

MEPHISTOPHILIS
Ay.

FAUSTUS
How many heavens, or spheres, are there?

MEPHISTOPHILIS
Nine: the seven planets, the firmament, and the empyreal
   heaven.

FAUSTUS
Well, resolve me in this question: Why have we not
   conjunctions, oppositions, aspects, eclipses, all at one
   time, but in some years we have more, in some less?

MEPHISTOPHILIS
Per inæqualem motum respecta totius.[1]

FAUSTUS
Well, I am answered. Tell me who made the world.

---

1 "On account of their unequal motion in relation to the whole."

MEPHISTOPHILIS
I will not.

FAUSTUS
Sweet Mephistophilis, tell me.

MEPHISTOPHILIS
Move me not, for I will not tell thee.

FAUSTUS
Villain, have I not bound thee to tell me anything?

MEPHISTOPHILIS
Ay, that is not against our kingdom; but this is.
Think thou on hell, Faustus, for thou art damn'd.

FAUSTUS
Think, Faustus, upon God that made the world.

MEPHISTOPHILIS
Remember this.

FAUSTUS
Ay, go, accursed spirit, to ugly hell.
'Tis thou hast damn'd distressed Faustus' soul.
Is't not too late?
    [*Re-enter* **GOOD ANGEL** *and* **EVIL ANGEL.**]

EVIL ANGEL
Too late.

GOOD ANGEL

Never too late, if Faustus can repent.

EVIL ANGEL

If thou repent, devils shall tear thee in pieces.

GOOD ANGEL

Repent, and they shall never raze thy skin.

[*Exeunt* **ANGELS**.]

FAUSTUS

Ah, Christ, my Savior,

Seek to save distressed Faustus' soul.

[*Enter* **LUCIFER**, **BELZEBUB**, and **MEPHISTOPHILIS**.]

LUCIFER

Christ cannot save thy soul, for he is just;

There's none but I have interest in the same.

FAUSTUS

O, who art thou that look'st so terrible?

LUCIFER

I am Lucifer,

And this is my companion-prince in hell.

FAUSTUS

O Faustus! they are come to fetch away thy soul!

LUCIFER

We come to tell thee thou dost injure us;
Thou talk'st of Christ contrary to thy promise;
Thou should'st not think of God: think of the Devil,
And of his dam, too.

FAUSTUS

Nor will I henceforth: pardon me in this,
And Faustus vows never to look to Heaven,
Never to name God, or to pray to him,
To burn his Scriptures, slay his ministers,
And make my spirits pull his churches down.

LUCIFER

Do so, and we will highly gratify thee. Faustus, we are
    come from hell to show thee some pastime. Sit down,
    and thou shalt see all the Seven Deadly Sins appear in
    their proper shapes.

FAUSTUS

That sight will be pleasing unto me,
As Paradise was to Adam the first day
Of his creation.

LUCIFER

Talk not of Paradise nor creation, but mark this show:
    talk of the Devil, and nothing else.—Come away!
    [*Enter the* **SEVEN DEADLY SINS**.]
Now, Faustus, examine them of their several names and
    dispositions.

FAUSTUS

What art thou—the first?

PRIDE

I am Pride. I disdain to have any parents. I am like to
    Ovid's flea: I can creep into every corner of a wench;
    sometimes, like periwig, I sit upon her brow; or like
    a fan of feathers, I kiss her lips; indeed I do—what
    do I not? But, fie, what a scent is here! I'll not speak
    another word, except the ground were perfum'd,
    and covered with cloth of arras.

FAUSTUS

What art thou—the second?

COVET

I am Covetousness, begotten of an old churl in an old
    leathern bag; and might I have my wish I would desire
    that this house and all the people in it were turn'd to
    gold, that I might lock you up in my good chest.
    O, my sweet gold!

FAUSTUS

What art thou—the third?

WRATH

I am Wrath. I had neither father nor mother: I leapt out of
    a lion's mouth when I was scarce half an hour old; and
    ever since I have run up and down the world with this

case[1] of rapiers wounding myself when I had nobody to fight withal. I was born in hell; and look to it, for some of you shall be my father.

Faustus

What art thou—the fourth?

Envy

I am Envy, begotten of a chimney sweeper and an oyster-wife. I cannot read, and therefore wish all books were burnt. I am lean with seeing others eat. O that there would come a famine through all the world, that all might die, and I live alone! then thou should'st see how fat i would be. But must thou sit and I stand! Come down with a vengeance!

Faustus

Away, envious rascal! What art thou—the fifth?

Gluttony

Who, I, sir? I am Gluttony. My parents are all dead, and the devil a penny they have left me, but a bare pension, and that is thirty meals a day and ten bevers[2]—a small trifle to suffice nature. O, I come of a royal parentage! My grandfather was a Gammon of Bacon, my grandmother a Hogshead of Claret-wine; my godfathers were these, Peter Pickleherring, and

---

1 Pair.
2 Refreshments between meals.

Martin Martlemas-beef.[1] O, but my godmother, she was a jolly gentlewoman, and well beloved in every good town and city; her name was Mistress Margery Marchbeer. Now, Faustus, thou hast heard all my progeny, wilt thou bid me to supper?

Faustus
No, I'll see thee hanged: thou wilt eat up all my victuals.

Gluttony
Then the Devil choke thee!

Faustus
Choke thyself, glutton! Who art thou—the sixth?

Sloth
I am Sloth. I was begotten on a sunny bank, where I have lain ever since; and you have done me great injury to bring me from thence: let me be carried thither again by Gluttony and Lechery. I'll not speak another word for a king's ransom.

Faustus
What are you, Mistress Minx, the seventh and last?

Lechery
Who, I, sir? I am one that loves an inch of raw mutton

---

1 Martlemas or Martinmas was the customary time for hanging up provisions to dry which had been salted for the winter.

better than an ell of fried stockfish; and the first letter
of my name begins with Lechery.

LUCIFER
Away to hell, to hell!   [*Exeunt the* **SINS**.]
—Now, Faustus, how dost thou like this?

FAUSTUS
O, this feeds my soul!

LUCIFER
Tut, Faustus, in hell is all manner of delight.

FAUSTUS
O might I see hell, and return again.
How happy were I then!

LUCIFER
Thou shalt; I will send for thee at midnight,
In meantime take this book; peruse it throughly,
And thou shalt turn thyself into what shape thou wilt.

FAUSTUS
Great thanks, mighty Lucifer!
This will I keep as chary, as my life.

LUCIFER
Farewell, Faustus, and think on the Devil.

FAUSTUS

Farewell, great Lucifer! Come, Mephistophilis.

[Exeunt omnes.]

[*Enter* **WAGNER**.]

WAGNER

Learned Faustus,
To know the secrets of astronomy,
Graven in the book of Jove's high firmament,
Did mount himself to scale Olympus' top,
Being seated in a chariot burning bright,
Drawn by the strength of yoky dragons' necks.
He now is gone to prove cosmography,
And, as I guess, will first arrive at Rome,
To see the Pope and manner of his court,
And take some part of holy Peter's feast,
That to this day is highly solemnis'd.

[Exit.]

Scene VII.

THE POPE'S PRIVY-CHAMBER.

[*Enter* FAUSTUS *and* MEPHISTOPHILIS.]

FAUSTUS
Having now, my good Mephistophilis,
Past with delight the stately town of Trier,[1]
Environ'd round with airy mountain-tops,
With walls of flint, and deep entrenched lakes,
Not to be won by any conquering prince;
From Paris next, coasting the realm of France,
We saw the river Maine fall into Rhine,
Whose banks are set with groves of fruitful vines;
Then up to Naples, rich Campania,
Whose buildings fair and gorgeous to the eye,
The streets straight forth, and pav'd with finest brick,
Quarter the town in four equivalents.
There saw we learned Maro's[2] golden tomb,
The way he cut, an English mile in length,
Thorough a rock of stone in one night's space;
From thence to Venice, Padua, and the rest,
In one of which a sumptuous temple stands,
That threats the stars with her aspiring top,

---

1 Treves.
2 Virgil, who was reputed a magician in the Middle Ages, was buried at Naples.

Thus hitherto has Faustus spent his time:
But tell me, now, what resting-place is this?
Hast thou, as erst I did command,
Conducted me within the walls of Rome?

MEPHISTOPHILIS
Faustus, have; and because we will not be unprovided,
    I have taken up[1] his Holiness' privy-chamber for
    our use.

FAUSTUS
I hope his Holiness will bid us welcome.

MEPHISTOPHILIS
Tut, 'tis no matter, man, we'll be bold with his good cheer.
And now, my Faustus, that thou mayst perceive
What Rome containeth to delight thee with,
Know that this city stands upon seven hills
That underprop the groundwork of the same.
[Just through the midst runs Aowing Tiber's stream,
With winding banks that cut it in two parts:]
Over the which four stately bridges lean,
That make safe passage to each part of Rome:
Upon the bridge call'd Ponto Angelo
Erected is a castle passing strong,
Within whose walls such store of ordnance are,
And double cannons, fram'd of carved brass,
As match the days within one complete year;

---

1 Engaged.

Besides the gates and high pyramides,
Which Julius Cæsar brought from Africa.

FAUSTUS
Now by the kingdoms of infernal rule,
Of Styx, of Acheron, and the fiery lake
Of ever-burning Phlegethon, I swear
That I do long to see the monuments
And situation of bright-splendent Rome:
Come therefore, let's away.

MEPHISTOPHILIS
Nay, Faustus, stay; I know you'd fain see the Pope,
And take some part of holy Peter's feast,
Where thou shalt see a troop of bald-pate friars,
Whose *summum bonum* is in belly-cheer.

FAUSTUS
Well, I'm content to compass then some sport,
And by their folly make us merriment.
Then charm me, [Mephistophilis,] that I
May be invisible, to do what I please
Unseen of any whilst I stay in Rome.
                    [**MEPHISTOPHILIS** *charms him.*]

MEPHISTOPHILIS
So, Faustus, now
Do what thou wilt, thou shalt not be discern'd.

[*Sound a sennet.*[1] *Enter the* **Pope** *and the* **Cardinal** *of* **Lorrain** *to the banquet, with* **Friars** *attending.*]

Pope

My Lord of Lorrain, wilt please you draw near?

Faustus

Fall to, and the devil choke you an[2] you spare!

Pope

How now! Who's that which spake?—Friars, look about.

1 Friar

Here's nobody, if it like your Holiness.

Pope

My lord, here is a dainty dish was sent me from the
    Bishop of Milan.

Faustus

I thank you, sir.   [*Snatches it.*]

Pope

How now! Who's that which snatch'd the meat from me?
    Will no man look? My Lord, this dish was sent me
    from the Cardinal of Florence.

---

1 A particular set of notes on the trumpet or cornet, different from a flourish.
2 If.

Faustus

You say true; I'll ha't.   [*Snatches it.*]

Pope

What, again! My lord, I'll drink to your Grace.

Faustus

I'll pledge your Grace.   [*Snatches the cup.*]

Cardinal Of Lorrain

My lord, it may be some ghost newly crept out of
    purgatory, come to beg a pardon of your Holiness.

Pope

It may be so. Friars, prepare a dirge to lay the fury of this
    ghost.
Once again, my lord, fall to.
                        [*The* **Pope** *crosseth himself.*]

Faustus

What, are you crossing of yourself? Well, use that trick no
    more I would advise you.
                        [*The* **Pope** *crosses himself again.*]
Well, there's the second time. Aware the third, I give you
    fair warning.
    [*The* **Pope** *crosses himself again, and* **Faustus** *hits him
    a box of the ear; and they all run away.*]
Come on, Mephistophilis, what shall we do?

MEPHISTOPHILIS

Nay, I know not. We shall be curs'd with bell, book, and
candle.

FAUSTUS

How! bell, book, and candle,—candle, book, and bell,
Forward and backward to curse Faustus to hell!
Anon you shall hear a hog grunt, a calf bleat, and an ass
bray,
Because it is Saint Peter's holiday.

[*Re-enter all the* **FRIARS** *to sing the Dirge.*]

1 FRIAR

Come, brethren, let's about our business with good
devotion,

They sing:

Cursed be he that stole away his Holiness' meat
from the table! *Maledicat Dominus!*[1]
Cursed be he that struck his Holiness a blow on
the face! *Maledicat Dominus!*
Cursed be he that took Friar Sandelo a blow on
the pate! *Maledicat Dominus!*
Cursed be he that disturbeth our holy dirge!
Maledicat Dominus!
Cursed be he that took away his Holiness' wine!
Maledicat Dominus! Et omnes sancti![2] *Amen!*

---

1 "May the Lord curse him."
2 "And all the saints."

[**MEPHISTOPHILIS** *and* **FAUSTUS** *beat the Friars, and fling fireworks among them: and so exeunt.*
[*Enter* **CHORUS**.]

CHORUS
When Faustus had with pleasure ta'en the view
Of rarest things, and royal courts of kings,
He stay'd his course, and so returned home;
Where such as bear his absence but with grief,
I mean his friends, and near'st companions,
Did gratulate his safety with kind words,
And in their conference of what befell,
Touching his journey through the world and air,
They put forth questions of Astrology,
Which Faustus answer'd with such learned skill,
As they admir'd and wond'red at his wit.
Now is his fame spread forth in every land;
Amongst the rest the Emperor is one,
Carolus the Fifth, at whose palace now
Faustus is feasted 'mongst his noblemen.
What there he did in trial of his art,
I leave untold—your eyes shall see perform'd.

[*Exit.*]

Scene VIII.

[Enter **Robin** *the Ostler with a book in his hand.*]

Robin

O, this is admirable! here I ha' stolen one of Dr. Faustus' conjuring books, and i' faith I mean to search some circles for my own use. Now will I make all the maidens in our parish dance at my pleasure, stark naked before me; and so by that means I shall see more than e'er I felt or saw yet.

[Enter **Ralph** *calling* **Robin**.]

Ralph

Robin, prithee come away; there's a gentleman tarries to have his horse, and he would have his things rubb'd and made clean. He keeps such a chafing with my mistress about it; and she has sent me to look thee out. Prithee come away.

Robin

Keep out, keep out, or else you are blown up; you are dismemb'red, Ralph: keep out, for I am, about a roaring piece of work.

Ralph

Come, what dost thou with that same book? Thou canst
    not read.

Robin

Yes, my master and mistress shall find that I can read, he
    for his forehead, she for her private study; she's born
    to bear with me, or else my art falls.

Ralph

Why, Robin, what book is that?

Robin

What book! Why, the most intolerable book for conjuring
    that e'er was invented by any brimstone devil.

Ralph

Canst thou conjure with it?

Robin

I can do all these things easily with it: first, I can make
    thee drunk with ippocras[1] at any tabern in Europe for
    nothing; that's one of my conjuring works.

Ralph

Our Master Parson says that's nothing.

---

1 Wine mixed with sugar and spices.

ROBIN

True, Ralph; and more, Ralph, if thou hast any mind to
   Nan Spit, our kitchenmaid, then turn her and wind
   her to thy own use.

RALPH

O brave Robin, shall I have Nan Spit, and to mine
   own use? On that condition I'll feed thy devil with
   horsebread as long as he lives, of free cost.

ROBIN

No more, sweet Ralph: let's go and make clean our
   boots, which lie foul upon our hands, and then
   to our conjuring in the Devil's name.   [*Exeunt.*]

Scene IX.

An Inn.

*[Enter **Robin** and **Ralph** with a silver goblet.]*

Robin

Come, Ralph, did not I tell thee we were for ever made
  by this Doctor Faustus' book? *Ecce signum*,[1] here's a
  simple purchase[2] for horsekeepers; our horses shall eat
  no hay as long as this lasts.
  *[Enter the **Vintner**.]*

Ralph

But, Robin, here comes the vintner.

Robin

Hush! I'll gull him supernaturally. Drawer, I hope all is
  paid: God be with you. Come, Ralph.

Vintner

Soft, sir; a word with you. I must yet have a goblet paid
  from you, ere you go.

_____

1 "Behold the sign."

2 Gain.

ROBIN

I, a goblet, Ralph; I, a goblet! I scorn you, and you are but
    a[1] &c. I, a goblet! search me.

VINTNER

I mean so, sir, with your favor.   *[Searches him.]*

ROBIN

How say you now?

VINTNER

I must say somewhat to your fellow. You, sir!

RALPH

Me, sir! me, sir! search your fill.

                        *[**VINTNER** searches him.]*

Now, sir, you may be ashamed to burden honest men with
    a matter of truth.

VINTNER

Well, t' one of you hath this goblet about you.

ROBIN

[Aside.] You lie, drawer, 'tis afore me.—Sirrah you, I'll
    teach ye to impeach honest men; stand by;—I'll scour
    you for a goblet!—stand aside you had best, I charge
    you in the name of Belzebub, *[Aside to **RALPH**.]* Look
    to the goblet, Ralph.

---

1 The abuse was left to the actor's inventiveness.

VINTNER

What mean you, sirrah?

ROBIN

I'll tell you what I mean. *Reads [from a book.]*
Sanctobulorum, Periphrasticon—Nay, I'll tickle you,
vintner. [*Aside to Ralph*] Look to the goblet, Ralph.
[*Reads*]. *Polypragmos Belseborams framanto pacostiphos
tostu, Mephistophilis, &c.*
[*Enter* MEPHISTOPHILIS, *sets squibs at their backs, and
then exit. They run about.*]

VINTNER

O nomine Domini![1] what meanest thou, Robin? Thou
hast no goblet.

RALPH

Peccatum peccatorum![2] Here's thy goblet, good vintner.
[*Gives the goblet to* VINTNER, *who Exit.*]

ROBIN

Misericordia pro nobis![3] What shall I do? Good Devil,
forgive me now, and I'll never rob thy library more.
[*Re-enter to them* MEPHISTOPHILIS.]

MEPHISTOPHILIS

Monarch of hell, under whose black survey

---

1 "In the name of the Lord."
2 "Sin of sins."
3 "Mercy on us."

Great potentates do kneel with awful fear,
Upon whose altars thousand souls do lie,
How am I vexed with these villains' charms?
From Constantinople am I hither come
Only for pleasure of these damned slaves.

ROBIN

How from Constantinople? You have had a great journey.
    Will you take sixpence in your purse to pay for your
    supper, and begone?

MEPHISTOPHILIS

Well, villains, for your presumption, I transform thee into
    an ape, and thee into a dog; and so begone.

[*Exit.*]

ROBIN

How, into an ape? That's brave! I'll have fine sport with
    the boys. I'll get nuts and apples enow.

RALPH

And I must be a dog—

ROBIN

I' faith thy head will never be out of the pottage pot.

[*Exeunt.*]

Scene X.

THE COURT OF THE EMPEROR.

[*Enter* EMPEROR, FAUSTUS, *and a* KNIGHT *with attendants.*]

EMPEROR

Master Doctor Faustus, I have heard strange report of
thy knowledge in the black art, how that none in my
empire nor in the whole world can compare with
thee for the rare effects of magic; they say thou hast a
familiar spirit, by whom thou canst accomplish what
thou list. This, therefore, is my request, that thou let
me see some proof of thy skill, that mine eyes may
be witnesses to confirm what mine ears have heard
reported; and here I swear to thee by the honor of
mine imperial crown, that, whatever thou doest,
thou shalt be no ways prejudiced or endamaged.

KNIGHT

[*Aside.*] I' faith he looks much like a conjuror.

FAUSTUS

My gracious sovereign, though I must confess myself
far inferior to the report men have published, and

nothing answerable[1] to the honor of your imperial
majesty, yet for that love and duty binds me thereunto,
I am content to do whatsoever your majesty shall
command me.

Emperor
Then, Doctor Faustus, mark what I shall say.
As I was sometime solitary set
Within my closet, sundry thoughts arose
About the honor of mine ancestors,
How they had won by prowess such exploits,
Cot such riches, subdued so many kingdoms,
As we that do succeed, or they that shall
Hereafter possess our throne, shall
(I fear me) ne'er attain to that degree
Of high renown and great authority;
Amongst which kings is Alexander the Great,
Chief spectacle of the world's pre-eminence,
The bright shining of whose glorious acts
Lightens the world with his[2] reflecting beams,
As, when I heard but motion[3] made of him,
It grieves my soul I never saw the man.
If, therefore, thou by cunning, of thine art
Canst raise this man from hollow vaults below,
Where lies entomb'd this famous conqueror,
And bring with him his beauteous paramour,
Both in their right shapes, gesture, and attire

---

1 Proportionate.

2 Its.

3 Mention.

They us'd to wear during their time of life,
Thou shalt both satisfy my just desire,
And give me cause to praise thee whilst I live.

FAUSTUS

My gracious lord, I am ready to accomplish your request
so far forth as by art, and power of my Spirit, I am able
to perform.

KNIGHT

[*Aside.*] I' faith that's just nothing at all.

FAUSTUS

But, if it like your Grace, it is not in my ability to present
before your eyes the true substantial bodies of those
two deceased princes, which long since are consumed
to dust.

KNIGHT

[*Aside.*] Ay, marry, Master Doctor, now there's a sign of
grace in you, when you will confess the truth.

FAUSTUS

But such spirits as can lively resemble Alexander and
his paramour shall appear before your Grace in
that manner that they best liv'd in, in their most
flourishing estate; which I doubt not shall sufficiently
content your imperial majesty.

EMPEROR

Go to, Master Doctor, let me see them presently.

KNIGHT

Do you hear, Master Doctor? You bring Alexander and his
    paramour before the Emperor!

FAUSTUS

How then, sir?

KNIGHT

I' faith that's as true as Diana turn'd me to a stag!

FAUSTUS

No, sir, but when Actæon died, he left the horns for you.
    Mephistophilis, begone.

                              [*Exit* **MEPHISTOPHILIS**.]

KNIGHT

Nay, an you go to conjuring, I'll begone.   [*Exit.*]

FAUSTUS

I'll meet with you anon for interrupting me so. Here they
    are my gracious lord.

    [*Re-enter* **MEPHISTOPHILIS** *and* **SPIRITS** *in the shape
    of* **ALEXANDER** *and his* **PARAMOUR**.]

EMPEROR

Master Doctor, I heard this lady while she liv'd had a wart or
    mole in her neck: how shall I know whether it be so or no?

FAUSTUS

Your Highness may boldly go and see.

[*Exeunt* Spirits.]

EMPEROR

Sure these are no spirits, but the true substantial bodies
    of those two deceased princes.

FAUSTUS

Will't please your Highness now to send for the knight
    that was so pleasant with me here of late?

EMPEROR

One of you call him forth.

[*Exit* Attendant.]

[*Re-enter the* **KNIGHT** *with a pair of horns on his head.*]

How now, sir knight! why I had thought thou had'st been
    a bachelor, but now I see thou hast a wife, that not
    only gives thee horns, but makes thee wear them.
    Feel on thy head.

KNIGHT

Thou damned wretch and execrable dog,
Bred in the concave of some monstrous rock,

How darest thou thus abuse a gentleman?
Villain, I say, undo what thou hast done!

FAUSTUS

O, not so fast, sir; there's no haste; but, good, are you
rememb'red how you crossed me in my conference
with the Emperor? I think I have met with you for it.

EMPEROR

Good Master Doctor, at my entreaty release him; he hath
done penance sufficient.

FAUSTUS

My gracious lord, not so much for the injury he off'red
me here in your presence, as to delight you with some
mirth, hath Faustus worthily requited this injurious
knight; which, being all I desire, I am content to
release him of his horns: and, sir knight, hereafter
speak well of scholars. Mephistophilis, transform
him straight. [**MEPHISTOPHILIS** *removes the horns.*]
Now, my good lord, having done my duty I humbly
take my leave.

EMPEROR

Farewell, Master Doctor; yet, ere you go,
Expect from me a bounteous reward.   [*Exeunt.*]

Scene XI.

[*Enter* FAUSTUS *and* MEPHISTOPHILIS.]

FAUSTUS
Now, Mephistophilis, the restless course
That Time doth run with calm and silent foot,
Short'ning my days and thread of vital life,
Calls for the payment of my latest years;
Therefore, sweet Mephistophilis, let us
Make haste to Wittenberg.

MEPHISTOPHILIS
What, will you go on horseback or on foot?

FAUSTUS
Nay, till I'm past this fair and pleasant green.
I'll walk on foot.
    [*Enter a* HORSE-COURSER.]

HORSE-COURSER
I have been all this day seeking one Master Fustian: mass,
    see where he is! God save you, Master Doctor!

Faustus

What, horse-courser! You are well met.

Horse-Courser

Do you hear, sir? I have brought you forty dollars for your
horse.

Faustus

I cannot sell him so: if thou likest him for fifty, take him.

Horse-Courser

Alas, sir, I have no more.—I pray you speak for me.

Mephistophilis

I pray you let him have him: he is an honest fellow, and he
has a great charge, neither wife nor child.

Faustus

Well, come, give me your money. [**Horse-Courser** *gives*
Faustus *the money.*] My boy will deliver him to you.
But I must tell you one thing before you have him;
ride him not into the water at any hand.

Horse-Courser

Why, sir, will he not drink of all waters?

Faustus

O yes, he will drink of all waters, but ride him not into
the water: ride him over hedge or ditch, or where thou
wilt, but not into the water.

HORSE-COURSER

Well, sir.—Now I am made man forever. I'll not leave
my horse for forty. [Aside] If he had but the quality of
hey-ding-ding, hey-ding-ding; I'd make a brave living
on him: he has a buttock as slick as an eel. Well, God
b' wi'ye, sir, your boy will deliver him me: but hark ye,
sir; if my horse be sick or ill at ease, if I bring his water
to you, you'll tell me what it is?

[*Exit* HORSE-COURSER.]

FAUSTUS

Away, you villain; what, dost think I am a horse-doctor?
What art thou, Faustus, but a in an condemn'd to die?
Thy fatal time doth draw to final end;
Despair doth drive distrust unto my thoughts:
Confound these passions with a quiet sleep:
Tush, Christ did call the thief upon the cross;

[*Sleeps in his chair.*]

Then rest thee, Faustus, quiet in conceit.

[*Re-enter* HORSE-COURSER, *all wet, crying.*]

HORSE-COURSER

Alas, alas! Doctor Fustian, quotha? Mass, Doctor Lopus[1]
was never such a doctor. Has given me a purgation
has purg'd me of forty dollars; I shall never see them
more. But yet, like an ass as I was, I would not be ruled
by him, for he bade me I should ride him into no

---

1 Dr. Lopez, physician to Queen Elizabeth, hanged in 1594 on the charge of
conspiring to poison the Queen.

water. Now I, thinking my horse had had some rare quality that he would not have had me known of, I, like a venturous youth, rid him into the deep pond at the town's end. I was no sooner in the middle of the pond, but my horse vanish'd away, and I sat upon a bottle of hay, never so near drowning in my life. But I'll seek out my Doctor, and have my forty dollars again, or I'll make it the dearest horse!—O, yonder is his snipper-snapper.—Do you hear? You hey-pass,[1] where's your master?

Mephistophilis
Why, sir, what would you? You cannot speak with him.

Horse-Courser
But I will speak with him.

Mephistophilis
Why, he's fast asleep. Come some other time.

Horse-Courser
I'll speak with him now, or I'll break his glass windows about his ears.

Mephistophilis
I tell thee he has not slept this eight nights.

---

1 A juggler's term, like "presto, Aly!" Hence applied to the juggler himself.

Horse-Courser

An he have not slept this eight weeks, I'll speak with him.

Mephistophilis

See where he is, fast asleep.

Horse-Courser

Ay, this is he. God save you, Master Doctor! Master
    Doctor, Master Doctor Fustian!—Forty dollars, forty
    dollars for a bottle of hay!

Mephistophilis

Why, thou seest he hears thee not.

Horse-Courser

So ho, ho!—So, ho, ho! [*Hollas in his ear.*] No, will you not
    wake? I'll make you wake ere I go. [*Pulls* **Faustus** *by
    the leg, and pulls it away.*] Alas, I am undone! What
    shall I do?

Faustus

O my leg, my leg! Help, Mephistophilis! call the officers.
    My leg, my leg!

Mephistophilis

Come, villain, to the constable.

Horse-Courser

O lord, sir, let me go, and I'll give you forty dollars more.

MEPHISTOPHILIS
Where be they?

HORSE-COURSER
I have none about me. Come to my ostry[1] and I'll give
    them you.

MEPHISTOPHILIS
Begone quickly.   [**HORSE-COURSER** *runs away.*]

FAUSTUS
What, is he gone? Farewell he! Faustus has his leg again,
    and the horse-courser, I take it, a bottle of hay for his
    labor. Well, this trick shall cost him forty dollars more.
    [*Enter* **WAGNER**.]
How now, Wagner, what's the news with thee?

WAGNER
Sir, the Duke of Vanholt doth earnestly entreat your
    company.

FAUSTUS
The Duke of Vanholt! an honorable gentleman, to
    whom I must be no niggard of my cunning. Come,
    Mephistophilis, let's away to him.
                                     [*Exeunt.*]

---

1 Inn.

Scene XII.

THE COURT OF THE DUKE OF VANHOLT.

[*Enter the* DUKE *of* VANHOLT, *the* DUCHESS, FAUSTUS, *and* MEPHISTOPHILIS.]

DUKE

Believe me, Master Doctor, this merriment hath much
   pleased me.

FAUSTUS

My gracious lord, I am glad it contents you so well.—But
   it may be, madam, you take no delight in this. I have
   heard that great-bellied women do long for some
   dainties or other. What is it, madam? Tell me, and
   you shall have it.

DUCHESS

Thanks, good Master Doctor; and for I see your courteous
   intent to pleasure me, I will not hide from you the
   thing my heart desires; and were it now summer, as
   it is January and the dead time of the winter, I would
   desire no better meat than a dish of ripe grapes.

FAUSTUS

Alas, madam, that's nothing! Mephistophilis, begone.
                            [*Exit* MEPHISTOPHILIS.]

Were it a greater thing than this, so it would content you,
you should have it.
[*Re-enter* **Mephistophilis** *with the grapes.*]
Here they be, madam; wilt please you taste on them?

Duke

Believe me, Master Doctor, this makes me wonder above
the rest, that being in the dead time of winter, and in the
month of January, how you should come by these grapes.

Faustus

If it like your Grace, the year is divided into two circles
over the whole world, that, when it is here winter with
us, in the contrary circle it is summer with them, as in
India, Saba, and farther countries in the East; and by
means of a swift spirit that have, I had them brought
hither, as ye see.—How do you like them, madam; be
they good?

Duchess

Believe me, Master Doctor, they be the best grapes that I
e'er tasted in my life before.

Faustus

I am glad they content you so, madam.

Duke

Come, madam, let us in, where you must well reward this
learned man for the great kindness he hath show'd to
you.

DUCHESS

And so I will, my lord; and whilst I live, rest beholding for
    this courtesy.

FAUSTUS

I humbly thank your Grace.

DUKE

Come, Master Doctor, follow us and receive your reward.

                                                 [*Exeunt.*]

Scene XIII.

A ROOM IN THE HOUSE OF FAUSTUS.

[*Enter* **Wagner**, *solus.*]

Wagner
I think my master means to die shortly,
For he hath given to me all his goods;
And yet, methinks, if that death were near,
He would not banquet and carouse and swill
Amongst the students, as even now he doth,
Who are at supper with such belly-cheer
As Wagner ne'er beheld in all his life.
See where they come! Belike the feast is ended.
　[*Enter* **Faustus**, *with two or three* **Scholars** *and*
　Mephistophilis.]

1 Scholar
Master Doctor Faustus, since our conference about fair
　ladies, which was the beautifullest in all the world, we
　have determined with ourselves that Helen of Greece
　was the admirablest lady that ever lived: therefore,
　Master Doctor, if you will do us that favor, as to let us
　see that peerless dame of Greece, whom all the world
　admires for majesty, we should think ourselves much
　beholding unto you.

Faustus

Gentlemen,
For that I know your friendship is unfeigned,
And Faustus' custom is not to deny
The just requests of those that wish him well,
You shall behold that peerless dame of Greece,
No otherways for pomp and majesty
Than when Sir Paris cross'd the seas with her,
And brought the spoils to rich Dardania.
Be silent, then, for danger is in words.

> [*Music sounds, and* Helen *passeth over the stage.*]

2 Scholar

Too simple is my wit to tell her praise,
Whom all the world admires for majesty.

3 Scholar

No marvel though the angry Greeks pursu'd
With ten years' war the rape of such a queen,
Whose heavenly beauty passeth all compare.

1 Scholar

Since we have seen the pride of Nature's works,
And only paragon of excellence.

> [*Enter an* Old Man.]

Let us depart; and for this glorious deed
Happy and blest be Faustus evermore.

Faustus
Gentlemen, farewell the same I wish to you.

> [*Exeunt* **Scholars** *and* **Wagner**].

Old Man
Ah, Doctor Faustus, that I might prevail
To guide thy steps unto the way of life,
By which sweet path thou mayst attain the goal
That shall conduct thee to celestial rest!
Break heart, drop blood, and mingle it with tears,
Tears falling from repentant heaviness
Of thy most vile and loathsome filthiness,
The stench whereof corrupts the inward soul
With such flagitious crimes of heinous sins
As no commiseration may expel,
But mercy, Faustus, of thy Savior sweet,
Whose blood alone must wash away thy guilt.

Faustus
Where art thou, Faustus? Wretch, what hast thou done?
Damn'd art thou, Faustus, damn'd; despair and die!
Hell calls for right, and with a roaring voice
Says "Faustus! come! thine hour is [almost] come!"
And Faustus [now] will come to do thee right.

> [**Mephistophilis** *gives him a dagger.*]

Old Man
Ah stay, good Faustus, stay thy desperate steps!
I see an angel hovers o'er thy head,

And, with a vial full of precious grace,
Offers to pour the same into thy soul:
Then calf for mercy, and avoid despair.

FAUSTUS
Ah, my sweet friend, I feel
Thy words do comfort my distressed soul.
Leave me a while to ponder on my sins.

OLD MAN
I go, sweet Faustus, but with heavy cheer,
Fearing the ruin of thy hopeless soul.   [*Exit.*]

FAUSTUS
Accursed Faustus, where is mercy now?
I do repent; and yet I do despair;
Hell strives with grace for conquest in my breast:
What shall I do to shun the snares of death?

MEPHISTOPHILIS
Thou traitor, Faustus, I arrest thy soul
For disobedience to my sovereign lord;
Revolt, or I'll in piecemeal tear thy flesh.

FAUSTUS
Sweet Mephistophilis, entreat thy lord
To pardon my unjust presumption,
And with my blood again I will confirm
My former vow I made to Lucifer.

MEPHISTOPHILIS

Do it now then quickly, with unfeigned heart,

Lest danger do attend thy drift.

    [**FAUSTUS** *stabs his arm and writes on a paper with his blood.*]

FAUSTUS

Torment, sweet friend, that base and crooked age,[1]

That durst dissuade me from my Lucifer,

With greatest torments that our hell affords.

MEPHISTOPHILIS

His faith is great, I cannot touch his soul;

But what I may afflict his body with

I will attempt, which is but little worth.

FAUSTUS

One thing, good servant, let me crave of thee,

To glut the longing of my heart's desire,—

That I might have unto my paramour

That heavenly Helen, which I saw of late,

Whose sweet embracings may extinguish clean

These thoughts that do dissuade me from my vow,

And keep mine oath I made to Lucifer.

MEPHISTOPHILIS

Faustus, this or what else thou shalt desire

Shall be perform'd in twinkling of an eye.

_____

1 Old man.

[*Re-enter* HELEN.]

FAUSTUS

Was this the face that launch'd a thousand ships,
And burnt the topless[1] towers of Ilium?
Sweet Helen, make me immortal with a kiss.

[*Kisses her.*]

Her lips suck forth my soul; see where it flies!—
Come, Helen, come, give me my soul again.
Here will I dwell, for Heaven be in these lips,
And all is dross that is not Helena.

[*Enter* OLD MAN.]

I will be Paris, and for love of thee,
Instead of Troy, shall Wittenberg be sack'd;
And I will combat with weak Menelaus,
And wear thy colors on my plumed crest;
Yea, I will wound Achilles in the heel,
And then return to Helen for a kiss.
Oh, thou art fairer than the evening air
Clad in the beauty of a thousand stars;
Brighter art thou than faming Jupiter
When he appear'd to hapless Semele:
More lovely than the monarch of the sky
In wanton Arethusa's azur'd arms:
And none but thou shalt be my paramour.

[*Exeunt.*]

---

1 Unsurpassed in height.

OLD MAN

Accursed Faustus, miserable man,

That from thy soul exclud'st the grace of Heaven,

And flyst the throne of his tribunal seat!

    [*Enter* **DEVILS**.]

Satan begins to sift me with his pride:

As in this furnace God shall try my faith,

My faith, vile hell, shall triumph over thee.

Ambitious fiends! see how the heavens smiles

At your repulse, and laughs your state to scorn!

Hence, hell! for hence I fly unto my God.

                                [*Exeunt.*]

Scene XIV.

THE SAME.

[*Enter* FAUSTUS *with the* SCHOLARS.]

FAUSTUS
Ah, gentlemen!

1 SCHOLAR
What ails Faustus?

FAUSTUS
Ah, my sweet chamber-fellow, had I lived with thee, then had I lived still! but now I die eternally. Look, comes he not, come he not?

2 SCHOLAR
What means Faustus?

3 SCHOLAR
Belike he is grown into some sickness by being over solitary.

1 SCHOLAR
If it be so, we'll have physicians to cure him. 'Tis but a surfeit. Never fear, man.

FAUSTUS

A surfeit of deadly sin that hath damn'd both body and soul.

2 SCHOLAR

Yet, Faustus, look up to Heaven; remember God's mercies
are infinite.

FAUSTUS

But Faustus' offences can never be pardoned: the serpent
that tempted Eve may be sav'd, but not Faustus. Ah,
gentlemen, hear me with patience, and tremble not
at my speeches! Though my heart pants and quivers
to remember that I have been a student here these
thirty years, oh, would I had never seen Wittenberg,
never read book! And what wonders I have done,
all Germany can witness, yea, the world; for which
Faustus hath lost both Germany and the world, yea
Heaven itself, Heaven, the seat of God, the throne of
the blessed, the kingdom of joy; and must remain in
hell for ever, hell, ah, hell, for ever! Sweet friends! what
shall become of Faustus being in hell for ever?

3 SCHOLAR

Yet, Faustus, call on God.

FAUSTUS

On God, whom Faustus hath abjur'd! on God, whom
Faustus hath blasphemed! Ah, my God, I would weep,
but the Devil draws in my tears. Gush forth blood
instead of tears! Yea, life and soul! Oh, he stays my

tongue! I would lift up my hands, but see, they hold
them, they hold them!

ALL
Who, Faustus?

FAUSTUS
Lucifer and Mephistophilis. Ah, gentlemen, I gave them
my soul for my cunning!

ALL
God forbid!

FAUSTUS
God forbade it indeed; but Faustus hath done it. For vain
pleasure of twenty-four years hath Faustus lost eternal
joy and felicity. I writ them a bill with mine own
blood: the date is expired; the time will come, and he
will fetch me.

1 SCHOLAR
Why did not Faustus tell us of this before, that divines
might have prayed for thee?

FAUSTUS
Oft have I thought to have done so; but the Devil
threat'ned to tear me in pieces if I nam'd God; to fetch
both body and soul if I once gave ear to divinity: and
now 't is too late. Gentlemen, away! lest you perish
with me.

2 SCHOLAR
Oh, what shall we do to save Faustus?

FAUSTUS
Talk not of me, but save yourselves, and depart.

3 SCHOLAR
God will strengthen me. I will stay with Faustus.

1 SCHOLAR
Tempt not God, sweet friend; but let us into the next
    room, and there pray for him.

FAUSTUS
Ay, pray for me, pray for me! and what noise soever ye
    hear, come not unto me, for nothing can rescue me.

2 SCHOLAR
Pray thou, and we will pray that God may have mercy
    upon thee.

FAUSTUS
Gentlemen, farewell! If I live till morning I'll visit you: if
    not—Faustus is gone to hell.

ALL
Faustus, farewell!
                    [*Exeunt* **SCHOLARS**. *The clock strikes eleven.*]

FAUSTUS

Ah, Faustus,

Now hast thou but one bare hour to live,

And then thou must be damn'd perpetually!

Stand still, you ever-moving spheres of Heaven,

That time may cease, and midnight never come;

Fair Nature's eye, rise, rise again and make

Perpetual day; or let this hour be but

A year, a month, a week, a natural day,

That Faustus may repent and save his soul!

O lente, lente, currite noctis equil![1]

The stars move still,[2] time runs, the clock will strike,

The Devil will come, and Faustus must be damn'd.

O, I'll leap up to my God! Who pulls me down?

See, see where Christ's blood streams in the firmament!

One drop would save my soul—Half a drop: ah, my
     Christ!

Ah, rend not my heart for naming of my Christ!

Yet will I call on him: o spare me, Lucifer!—

Where is it now? 'Tis gone; and see where God

Stretcheth out his arm, and bends his ireful brows!

Mountain and hills come, come and fall on me,

And hide me from the heavy wrath of God!

No! no!

Then will I headlong run into the earth;

Earth gape! O no, it will not harbor me!

You stars that reign'd at my nativity,

---

1 "Run softly, softly, horses of the night." - Ovid's Amores, i. 13.

2 Without ceasing.

Whose influence hath allotted death and hell,
Now draw up Faustus like a foggy mist
Into the entrails of yon laboring clouds,
That when they vomit forth into the air,
My limbs may issue from their smoky mouths,
So that my soul may but ascend to Heaven.

                              [*The watch strikes the half hour*].

Ah, half the hour is past! 'Twill all be past anon!
O God!
If thou wilt not have mercy on my soul,
Yet for Christ's sake whose blood hath ransom'd me,
Impose some end to my incessant pain;
Let Faustus live in hell a thousand years—
A hundred thousand, and at last be sav'd!
O, no end is limited to damned souls!
Why wert thou not a creature wanting soul?
Or why is this immortal that thou hast?
Ah, Pythagoras metempsychosis! were that true,
This soul should fly from me, and I be chang'd
Unto some brutish beast! All beasts are happy,
For, when they die,
Their souls are soon dissolv'd in elements;
But mine must live, still to be plagu'd in hell.
Curst be the parents that engend'red mel
No, Faustus: curse thyself: curse Lucifer
That hath depriv'd thee of the joys of Heaven.

                              [*The clock striketh twelve.*]

O, it strikes, it strikes! Now, body, turn to air,
Or Lucifer will bear thee quick to hell.

                              [*Thunder and lightning.*]

O soul, be chang'd into little water-drops,
And fall into the ocean—ne'er be found.
My God! my God! look not so fierce on me!
    [*Enter* DEVILS.]
Adders and serpents, let me breathe awhile!
Ugly hell, gape not! come not, Lucifer!
I'll burn my books!—Ah Mephistophilis!

                        [*Exeunt* DEVILS *with* FAUSTUS.]
    [*Enter* CHORUS.]

CHORUS
Cut is the branch that might have grown full straight,
And burned is Apollo's laurel bough,
That sometimes grew within this learned man.
Faustus is gone; regard his hellish fall,
Whose fiendful fortune may exhort the wise
Only to wonder at unlawful things,
Whose deepness doth entice such forward wits
To practice more than heavenly power permits.

                                    [*Exit.*]

Terminat hora diem, terminat author opus.[1]

---

1 "The hour ends the day, the author ends his work."

Printed in the USA
CPSIA information can be obtained
at www.ICGtesting.com
JSHW012042140824
68134JS00033B/3216

9 781722 503819